To Bobby, with love and gratitude

Never overlook what you see, for you will never see it again.

ROBIN BECKWITH

ISBN-978-1-934005-03-3
ISBN-978-1-934005-04-0

Greenwood Valley Press
Stafford, Texas 77477
Library of Congress Control Number: 2023900911
Printed in the United States of America

CONTENTS

XI

Selected Writings of an Obscure Woman

Volume I: Stories

Robin Beckwith

WHAT IS ART?

Normally I would have gone by the duck pond, but today I could not. I usually took bread for the ducks. I would watch as others unleashed their dogs, who then went bellyflopping into the water, bounding after some floatable object, bringing it eagerly and wetly back to their owners' feet. It was selfish of me, but I had just taken on a client who snatched at my hours as greedily as the ducks did the bread. I had been hesitant because I did not like her art. She mostly concentrated on the female form, painting it in dark tones splintered into myriad glass-edged shards. That was one series. Another showed female figures rippling still and darkly under water.

She was a big woman, not fat, but tall and robust. She wanted a card. She wanted galleries' names. She wanted a website and brochure. Even my doorbell seemed to ring with more insistence whenever she arrived. She was forty. She had never tried publicity before, but one of her friends suggested that was why her success was so slim, and she had bounded like one of the pond dogs at the idea of wider fame.

"My mother loves my work," she said. "I thought she wouldn't. I was afraid to show it to her. And she said—well I was twenty-nine then—and she said, 'Well, it's dark, isn't it. But then some truths are.'"

"Bleak?"

"Bleak?" she snapped. "Of course! Beauty is, when it comes to that."

I had to fight hard not to see myself in her shards, not to cry out as her naked glass-shattered paint pierced my skin.

One day I found myself saying in response to a remark she made: "Of course I love my husband."

"Then," she said, "why do you look at my breasts?"

I was flustered. "I didn't know I did."

"You're more attracted to women than you think."

"I think it's possible to love the female form and not..." I stopped.

"Not what."

"Not be a lesbian."

"How naive you are."

"It's not easy living with anyone."

"How naive you are."

I was silent. I did not want her to balk at my bill. I worked hard for her. The website had drawn collectors in, the brochure had intrigued them.

"Maybe you're right," I lied.

"Not *maybe*, honey."

She did not see how her work stabbed at one's eyes. That was the nature of art, I guess. You saw your vision, but you didn't see what it meant to others. Of course, did I really see more than she?

I thought of my husband's body and wished I was an artist who could render his form as breathing and whole as hers of women was eerie and fragmented. But real talent for drawing escaped me.

However, I could photograph. My husband was reluctant. I wanted to try, though.

My client said, "Honey, I do not hesitate to use my lovers as my models."

I wondered how she survived their sharp edges. But it was only art.

"By the time I get them on canvas," she said, "I'm bored with them."

"You've used them up," I ventured.

"Quite so," she said. "Maybe it'll happen to you."

We had been married twenty years.

In the afterglow one lazy afternoon, I got out the camera and enticed my husband to my studio. I oiled his body and photographed him by the light of naked bulbs and candles. I couldn't stop.

I rolled the full-length mirror out. Which was him and which the image? We were there for hours.

We came back again and again for weeks. There was no angle, I thought, I did not see.

When I looked at the images, I was amazed. I could not imagine collectors would reject such a strongly masculine beauty.

I conducted my publicity campaign much as I had for my client. Galleries responded. They wanted to meet the artist.

They saw me and were disappointed.

You're a woman, they said.

Well, yes.

They couldn't believe it. It's such a masculine view, they said.

They didn't know if they could market the images as photographed by a woman. The subject, maybe, but not the artist.

I lied. I said he was bisexual.

That intrigued them.

The shades of gray that mask our love of male and female. Lust. Coyness. How did they put it? "The sheer beauty of the chiaroscuro of the skin—taut and muscular, with a mixture of brutal force and feminine grace." Yes, yes!! That was it!

My husband was amazed. Of course, he was unrecognizable. I made sure with shades and shadows and filters and framing.

He began to look at men differently. He saw sometimes their eyes caressing his body.

"Is it all right?" he asked me.

"Is what all right?"

"To be caught in this, in this, well, *web of eyes*. All eyeing each other. Looking each other up and down."

I had no answer.

* * *

But my client. Her success was so much greater.

Women naked and shattered, drowning: Somehow, people needed to see that more.

FRIENDS

When you choose a friend, you start stepping into their moral universe and they into yours. What they sanction and what you sanction slowly become the boundaries of that relation. Either side may feel afraid to step into what they perceive may be danger.

She had thought this through carefully. Some people, she thought, were so needy they drained you of goodwill. Others were circumspect.

Would it be better, she thought, to invite an acquaintance and his wife to dinner and scare them off forever, or leave the relation pristine and arrested? What if there were something about her husband they didn't like? What if she didn't like his wife? What if they didn't like the way she treated her son?

The people they got to know were their son's friends' parents. These were people who held block parties. Susan and Henry wanted to know their neighbors, so they always participated. There was an odd collection of people in their neighborhood. About half were in their seventies and eighties. There were a few with children in college. The rest—no matter whether in their twenties, thirties, or forties—had children aged five or under.

There were a couple of neighbors who slapped their children. They avoided talking to them. But apparently one of these couples —Judy and Sam—had taken a liking to Stephen, their son. They had a son, a year younger than Stephen. Zach's eyes were large and silent and his hair was cropped unevenly close to his scalp.

At a late afternoon Sunday barbecue, Judy said to the small

group around her that "she cut it herself." A mother quickly picked up her wandering two-year-old and placed him on a safety swing. More people moved slowly over towards the swings.

"What did I say?" whispered Judy to Susan.

"Maybe Zach'll become a great general," said Susan.

"You think it looks military?"

"It's not the style they're wearing."

"It's not an easy thing to cut hair," said Judy.

Her son was throwing stones into the pond in the middle of the park.

Stephen clung to his mother's leg as the two women talked. He watched as Zach's stones scared off the ducks.

"Mom, could I have a bun for the ducks?"

Susan looked at Zachary, then at Judy.

"OK," she answered.

She watched as her son walked over to Zachary and bent down to talk closely to him. Zach continued throwing stones into the water. Stephen gave him half the bun.

Judy's mother watched too. "All the ducks do is shit and breed. That's what my husband says."

Susan continued with her eyes on the two boys. "The ducks are wild. It's good to have some wild animals in the middle of a big city."

"Sam's a crack shot. He wants to shoot them."

"He likes to hunt?"

"Yes. But he says now it's a rich man's sport."

But you live around here, you can afford a house here, thought Susan. She watched as her son threw pieces of the bun at the ducks. Zachary had stopped throwing stones and was watching Stephen. Then he tore off some of the hamburger bun Stephen had given him and threw little pieces to the ducks.

"Sam," Judy said, pointing towards the other end of the park. "I hope he doesn't see what Zach is doing."

The hamburger bun gone, the two boys ran towards the jungle gym and started climbing the slide.

Sam walked towards Susan and his wife. He reached out his

hand to shake Susan's. "Did you see that? Feeding those things? Was that *my* son?"

Susan was silent.

Judy looked afraid.

"It wasn't my idea," she said.

"I should hope not," said her husband.

"It's nice to share the park with other species. In my opinion," said Susan.

"I guess you're one of those nature freaks," he said with a slight smile.

"No. Big city girl. Hate to camp."

"Well, they'd be great for eating, they get so fat on all the food people give them. In *my* opinion, ma'am. Come on, Jude."

It was close to six-thirty.

"I got a hamburger for you just the way you like it," said Judy.

"Hey!" he yelled back as he strode off after Zachary. "That's what I pay you for."

No, she did not like these people. Susan watched as Sam abruptly picked up Zach and carried him away from the jungle gym. Stephen stared after them. The two boys waved to each other, Zachary hanging over his father's shoulder.

Susan said good-bye to Judy as she walked towards Stephen.

As she passed Sam carrying Zach, Sam shook his head and said, "Just about as hard as looking after a dog."

Susan had no time to reply. As she and Sam walked in opposite directions, she heard Zach say, "But we've *got* a dog."

Susan crouched down to her son and stroked his head. "You're a good boy."

Stephen was silent, looking after Zach and his parents walking out of the park.

"Zach's mom bakes lemon pie," Stephen said finally, walking slowly back to the barbecue with his mother.

"Your favorite."

Stephen was a quiet boy, the oldest of the neighborhood children, who seemed respected by them. Susan listened when he invited others over or when she observed him in a group. When he spoke, he spoke definitely. He could play with any boy he liked, but he did not seem to have close friends. Occasionally, he'd visit other kids' homes. Now he included Zachary's home, while the other children did not.

"It's hard to have friends when your name is Zachary," Stephen said one day.

Another time he said, "I told Zach's Mom not to cut his hair so short."

But his request didn't seem to have any effect.

"Zach almost always wears the same thing. Zach's Mom says she buys on special."

Susan said, "Well, I do, too."

Stephen nodded, "I know."

A couple of years went by. Stephen was not the oldest anymore. A nine-year-old boy had moved in three houses down. Stephen was seven. This other boy knew things, like how to play chess and the piano. Stephen wanted to learn, too. So the other boy, Alan, took on the task of teaching him.

Susan was amazed at how quickly Stephen caught on. She signed him up with Alan's piano teacher. The two boys practiced on Alan's piano, while Stephen begged to have one of his own. Susan and her husband discussed it with his teacher and managed to find an old upright that needed reconditioning.

Zachary came by looking for Stephen. It was difficult for Susan to say he was playing with Alan.

Zachary said slowly, "I miss him."

"You can come in, if you like."

The boy stood hesitant at the door. Susan reached out her hand and took hold of his. The young boy's palm was sweaty.

"Please, come in."

Zachary went with her into the kitchen.

"I can't have anything to eat or it might spoil my dinner," he said solemnly.

"How about a glass of milk?" asked Susan, watching as the boy gingerly sat on one of the chairs.

"I guess that would be OK," he said. His head was almost bald.

"Thank you, ma'am."

"Our old dog died," he said. "My Dad says maybe we can get a puppy if I'm a good boy."

He was silent as he drank his milk. Susan sat opposite him.

"I don't know if I'm good," he said.

The front door opened and Stephen raced into the kitchen, yelling, "I beat him! I beat him! Alan says he's mortified."

He stopped at the door to the kitchen.

"Oh, hi Zach." He stared at Zachary. "I don't know what mortified is."

"It's just about what you're feeling right now," said his mother.

"Oh," said Stephen. "Do you want me to teach you chess, Zach?"

"No."

"Why not? It's a great game."

"It's for pansies."

"What's that?"

"Men who do bad things."

Stephen looked at his mother. "I thought pansies were flowers." She nodded.

"My Dad says it's for men who do bad things," said Zach.

Stephen was silent.

"Did you see my piano?"

"I don't want to see your piano. It's for pansies, too."

"Alan's great," said Stephen. "You'd really like him."

"My Dad says he's a pansy and never to go there. Or else."

"Or else what?"

"Or else is very bad. I never got 'or else.'"

Stephen looked puzzled. "I can't see you cause I got to practice. Would it be a pansy thing to listen?"

"Dunno," said Zachary, staring down at his milk.

"Stay right there. Just pretend I never came in. Just pretend it's the radio," said Stephen, running into the living-room. Soon a simple melody filtered into the kitchen.

Susan watched Zach from the corner of her eye as Stephen's music surrounded them. Throughout his playing, Zach sat still and attentive, his eyes gradually filling with tears, until one escaped and streaked down his cheek.

When Stephen finished the piece, Zach got up and walked into the living-room. He went up to Stephen and kissed him on the cheek. Then he went to the front door and let himself out.

A few months later, Zachary and his family moved away. Judy was pregnant. Before they left, Susan met Judy at the grocery store.

"We're moving to a small town in Utah," she said sadly.

"Sam was promoted?"

"No. Another job. Selling vacuums wholesale. Seems like Utah's a growth territory."

"Stephen'll miss Zachary."

"Yes," said Judy. "He was a breath of fresh air. You must be a good mother."

"Well, I'm sure you are, too."

"Zach's head," Judy said. "I want you to know *I* never shaved it." She looked sad and drawn. "I hope the next one's a girl."

"Did Zach ever get his puppy?"

"Yes. It wasn't a collie like he wanted. It was one of those wiener dogs."

"Dachshunds."

"Yeah, dachshund. Zach took to him fine. He's looking after him like he was a prince."

That was the last they ever heard of Zach and his parents and their unborn child.

A couple of months after they left, Stephen said, "You could teach him things."

Susan hugged him. "He won't forget you. He won't forget."

GLANCING LIFE

S andra met George. They went for coffee. Actually, one regular café latte and one decaf cappuccino. And biscotti. They discussed life for two hours, sent out wedding invitations the next day, had a big expensive wedding because Mom wanted it, and saved themselves (without interest) for their wedding night because that was the right thing to do.

Lacking the down payment for a house because the money went for the wedding and honeymoon (six seasick days on a Caribbean cruise, with Pepto Bismol for dinner and separate bunks), she worked in the business world for two years, while he got an MBA, fabricated a plausible résumé, and landed a position with a corporate entity.

They stopped trying to have sex for fun and started trying to have sex to make a baby. They tried and tried and in spite of schedule conflicts managed to convince one intrepid sperm to get up the courage to commingle with a soft and shapely egg. When Junior emerged after nine months' cozy incubation in Sandra's womb into the School of Hard Knocks, Sandra quit her day job to work as a Mom.

Now cognizant of how personal commitment can turn backbone into jelly while ratcheting up fear and aggression in the workplace, George became a good team player at the firm.

After three sessions with a therapist stipulated by George's medical plan, Sandra was pronounced cured of her post-partum depression.

George and Sandra, who planned to have children quickly

because it worked in better with their retirement goals, tried and tried again, and finally got another egg to succumb to the charms of a dapper sperm.

With the kids out of her system, Sandra got her tubes tied, convinced George to get an au pair girl, and started her own company at home, trading in coffee futures, often working late into the night buying and selling on the internet, establishing a flourishing business, which she hid from George fearing his jealousy.

Junior and his sister learned to play the computer keyboard before they could talk, observed George in close consultation with the au pair girl late into the night, were diagnosed as codependently hyperactive by the age of three, sublimated into good obsessive-compulsive neurotics within the next two years, were inventing nightmarish interactive war simulation games by the time they were six, slept through school, threw mashed potatoes at George and Sandra when they were thirteen and fourteen, settled down by dyeing their hair green and purple and wearing sweatshirts saying "kill," and graduated from high school summa cum laude and unable to read and write. Junior joined an evangelical mission that had set up a software firm in Zamboanga. His sister became a mechanic and married her best friend's girlfriend.

George was finally laid off from the firm. Sandra confessed she'd made a lot of money in her business. George confessed he'd screwed the au pair girl. They sulked for two years. Then Sandra suggested they buy a coffeehouse franchise with the money she'd saved. So now they have a healthy business selling coffee: No latte, no espresso, no cappuccino, and no biscotti.

Disillusioned with the mission, Junior enrolled in a remedial reading class, discovered he had a brain, and started talking in complete sentences. Now a top aerospace mechanic, his sister managed to break up her marriage by discovering makeup and starting to wax her legs. Each found a good therapist, paid for her out of their own pockets because they felt insurance companies had no right to determine their level of mental health, and finally each independently got up enough courage to confront George and Sandra with their vapid lives.

George and Sandra were so shocked that after hours late into the night they can now be seen sitting together in their coffeehouse lingering over a cup of java, talking about life. Sometimes they hold hands and look at each other.

JANCY

It was a dark night. Not dark and *stormy*. Just dark. And I'm not stupid. I know the original comes from some novel out of the nineteenth century. It's dark because it's cloudy, which you really can't tell because, as I said, it's night, which by definition *is* dark. But anyway, you can figure it's cloudy because when you look at the sky you can't see stars or the moon or anything.

So I'm walking along this road, a dirt road. I could tell because of how it felt under my feet. Well, I have my Nikes on, but still you can tell there's gravel and stuff and that softer feel of earth instead of asphalt.

I'm looking for a horse. *My* horse. Some idiot left the gate to her enclosure open and she'd gotten out. So naturally I have to go looking for her. Actually it was not just *some* idiot, it was my cousin, who's *definitely* an idiot, who left the gate open. His brain is of course the size you normally get for humans. But since his ego takes up most of the space, there's not much left over for thinking. So he says things like, "Well, why'dja want a horse for anyway? All that money for hay. And then you got all that trouble of brushing it and taking care of it and everything." That's his lame way of getting out of admitting he was a real shithead for being so careless.

So I'm walking down this dirt road. It's about eleven o'clock. PM. And I'm looking for Jancy. That's my horse. I was going to call her Janet after this girl I know. But my Mom's name is Nancy. So I sort of put them together. She's the best horse you could ever know. Real sensitive and gentle. She's got good taste, too. There are certain people she just walks away from. My cousin Brent is one of them. I mean, he's the type of person that thinks "Brent" is a cool name. She'll snort and swish her tail a bit and walk over to something more interesting.

I figure I know where Jancy would go. She likes real sweet clover. You can tell. She gets real eager when there's some of it around. She lets it grow for awhile. She'll sniff at it, you know, and let it get till it's just right. Then, bang, it's gone. Like some treat she saves up for herself. I used to bring her some when I saw how much she liked it. But she'd sniff at it and mostly just leave it alone. That's how I knew she was checking out the clover, letting it grow till it got just to where it was how she likes it. Jancy's smart.

My Mom is smart, too. I mean, she *was*. I keep saying that. Talking like she's still around. Which she isn't. That's how come I'm living in the country. Cause she had this tumor—just a little one, really—on her brain. They took it off, you know, in an operation. She just didn't get well.

We'd visit her and you could tell she was trying real hard to get better. Putting on makeup and a nice robe and sitting up in a chair and smiling. She'd say, "Oh, I think I feel stronger today." And you knew she was *trying* to feel stronger. Making herself walk.

And my Dad brought her her favorite chocolates so she could fatten up a bit cause she got so thin. She would take his hand and cup her cheek into it and kiss it. Real tender. My Dad and I would leave and we'd be crying down the hall all the way to the car cause we missed her and we hated the hospital and we knew things didn't look good but you weren't allowed to say that.

I can hear all these crickets and sometimes an owl. And my feet crunching in the gravel and dirt. I have a flashlight with me but I don't have it on cause there's nothing to see anyway. I mean, I turned it on a few times, but whenever I did the little light just made the dark darker somehow cause it made these strange forms and shadows and all. It gave me the creeps so I just kept it off. Like maybe sometimes you just gotta accept it's dark and that's it. Somehow it makes me feel better. Like I just blend into the night.

Anyway, I know I'll *hear* Jancy. I don't need to see her to

15

know she's there. And she'll know it's me and come up to me real calm and then we'll go back.

My eye still hurts and my lip still hurts and my stomach still hurts. That Brent is a triple asshole. I'm fifteen and I'm small for my age. He's sixteen and got all these muscles and no neck cause he plays football.

Football. That's got to be one of the stupidest things ever invented. I know all the rules cause you can't exist as a teenage boy in America without knowing all that. But it seems like it's just one big excuse so you can ram into guys and break their ribs and grunt and pile up on a guy like you'd want to bury him. Or watch other guys do that.

The only time I like football is when I watch the sports news and they show you one right after the other all the times when one guy breaks away, clasping the ball and running like crazy and missing all those idiots that'd like to kill him.

My aunt put ice on my eye and my lip. You know, wrapped the ice in a dishtowel. She wasn't too sympathetic. She doesn't like my having Jancy. You can tell. She doesn't come out and say so. But she says, "That horse sure eats a lot, Burt." That's my uncle. But he doesn't care.

I don't know why he puts up with her. She's always saying how much stuff costs and how she got this real cheap. I hate it when anybody says something's real cheap. Just cause it didn't cost a lot doesn't mean to say it's *cheap*, if you know what I mean. And I'm not saying money's not important. But you don't have to be talking about how much things cost all the time. It makes you feel bad about using toilet paper or getting another glass of milk or something.

I just keep walking kind of slow and even and calm. I smell the wheat in the still soft air. It's maybe another mile, which isn't much to a horse.

Nobody said, "Hey, let's go look for Jancy" when they heard she'd gotten out. My uncle Burt was real tired and told me to calm down and it'd be OK. He was real nice, but he wasn't too eager to jump in the truck and go after a horse on a hunch I knew where she was when it was nine o'clock at night and he needed to get up at four. He said he would if I really wanted to, if it would make me feel better.

But my aunt Marcie said, "Burt, you need your sleep. You don't need to go off on some wild goose chase." Like it's not a *goose*, it's a *horse*. And not even a *wild* horse.

My aunt Marcie doesn't like it when I talk back. She always tells me to "quit being smart." That's such a stupid thing to say. I guess most people get told that when they're kids. Like it really does a lot of good in this world *not* to be smart. What I think is most people don't know *how* to be smart. Like they don't really know what smart *is*. Which I think is maybe why you got so many people that other people *think* are smart who really only just know a lot of stuff, you know, *information*, but they're not really *smart*.

My Mom is smart. *Was* smart. And my Dad. And Janet. She's small for her age, too. The teachers were real eager to put her ahead to the next grade, cause they figured it'd be more of a challenge for her, you know.

But her parents said to let her be a kid and she's already small and she'll just feel smaller. Which is stupid cause she's always been small and she'll always be small even when she's grown up. So what difference does it make? She's used to it. Her parents are tall and I bet when she heard what they said, *that*'s what made her feel small, not going ahead a grade, which she was looking forward to.

She wants to be a doctor. She's not sure what kind. Her parents are artists. Her Mom's a poet and her Dad's a painter. "Without art the fabric of society has no integrity." That's what Janet said her Mom said.

Janet's a real good writer, but she said she's afraid she'll miss too much if she just writes about everything, like in a diary. Like she won't really *live*, she'll just *write* about living. Maybe she'll just write in her spare time and heal people for her real work. That's what she says. But she's real quiet about it.

"The integrity of art has no fabric without society," Janet said.

But she'd never tell her Mom that. You just have to kind of shut up around her Mom. And it's funny cause she's so passionate about how you should be free to express yourself.

Janet says her parents are famous, but so what. She doesn't hardly like any poem her Mom writes, and there's only one or two paintings her Dad did that she really likes. She says maybe it's stuff you can only like if you're grown up. When I grow up I hope it doesn't mean I get bad taste and forget beauty.

Like this night. The soft breeze and the crickets and the frogs chirping. I hear an owl again and a flutter of wings. It's getting cooler and it seems even darker.

After the road, I walk across a couple of pretty muddy fields and through a bit of woods. Now there's the road again. And it's weird cause a truck went whizzing by and it's just a real small country road.

When I heard it, I hoped it would be my Dad. He writes me that he'll be coming by for me anytime now. Almost got enough money so we can at least rent a house, he says. But I don't know, he's been saying that for almost a year and I figure, well, I just gotta grow up and face facts that maybe I'll just never see him again.

Aunt Marcie just purses her lips whenever I get a letter from him. You can tell she doesn't like him. I tell myself that whatever she thinks doesn't count nearly so much as what uncle Burt thinks cause he's my Mom's brother. Sometimes Dad sends me money, which aunt Marcie can always tell is in there and she makes me hand it over to her.

"It's only our due, Burt," she says when my uncle shakes his head.

Whenever I hear a truck or a car, I always think it could be my Dad. I'd just jump in and go. Naturally we'd get Jancy and put her in a stall behind the truck. But I'd only say good-bye to my uncle. I want that more than money or being liked or anything.

I can see the red taillights disappear over a small rise in the road. Anyway it was going in the wrong direction. He could be lost, though. Or he might have stopped by the farm and they looked in my room and I wasn't there and he went out searching for me. Maybe he was worried.

I walk faster. But I soon lose the sound of the truck. It was going pretty fast to be looking for me anyway. A blur and like I couldn't tell what kind of truck it was.

Sometimes I think maybe he won't come by truck or car, but maybe on a bus. So I go down to the bus stop and watch all these buses going from here to there. The drivers all know me. It's nice when they say, "Hey, missed you last week." There's usually somebody that gets off. But it's never my Dad.

So pretty soon I'm at the place where I'd ridden with Jancy where she finds that real sweet clover the way she likes it. And I hear something that's kind of like it might be a horse. But it's kind of a wheezing sound. And I'm sort of worried.

I call out softly and then I hear back this wheezing sound that's trying to be loud and strong but just isn't. It's coming from over near a tree, which now I can see cause all of a sudden the clouds are wisped away and the moon is shining big and full.

Jancy's on the ground and my heart is pounding so hard I can't hear anything except for her wheezing tired and slow. I rush over to her and stroke her and she's all wet and I'm not stupid I know it's blood. There are tire marks right next to her in the soft earth near where the clover is.

I stay with Jancy and talk to her and talk to her about how there's this sweet bird that soars into the aquamarine shimmers in the summer sun that she can fly with like that horse in Greek mythology and she can see with it the joining of space and time through ceaseless wings and eyes that pierce colors through black black forever night forever day.

When the light comes I can hear a truck. I'm numb and Jancy's stopped wheezing. It stops on the road where it bends just where the clump of clover is and I look over and see my uncle Burt climb down from the truck. He walks towards me and takes my hand and pulls me up like I'm a little boy.

I hold him and hold him and cry and cry and he just strokes my head and clasps me to him. He picks me up and carries me bloody you can't tell what's blood and what's tears, opens the truck door, and sets me down.

He moves the truck back a bit from the road. Then he gets out a shovel from the back and just digs and digs until there's a hole big enough for Jancy. Then he shoves and shoves and eventually pushes her in and calls to me to come over. He gives me a shovel and we throw all the clover earth onto Jancy. It's so sweet and fragrant, the earth and the clover.

My uncle says, "Couldn't pick a better place for her."

He looks at me and strokes my head. I say good-bye to Jancy.

We walk back to the truck and I notice there's a dent in the front and some brown stuff any idiot would know was blood. My uncle shakes his head. He narrows his eyes and makes a fist. He just stands there like he would be frozen.

Then all of a sudden he punches the dent real hard. "Goddamn it!" he says. "God fucking damn it!"

Uncle Burt doesn't talk like that, so I'm real quiet. But I can't talk anyway, like to make a sound would hurt so bad it'd come out like blood.

When we got back Brent was looking real sulky at me.

Aunt Marcie said, "You aren't really going to make him pay back the whole price of a new horse, Burt."

She said it like an order.

Uncle Burt looked her square in the eye and said, "Yes, ma'am. Yes, ma'am, I sure am."

"Well, we'll just see about that," says my aunt.

"Yes we will, Marcie. We sure will."

And he told her a lot of stuff about how she can't protect her son from the realities of life and how it's wrong what he did and how if he doesn't learn now he'll never learn. Then they realized they were talking in front of us and they went up to their bedroom where you could hear the sound of their voices the rest of the day.

Brent wouldn't look at me. It's funny I know but I kinda felt sorry for him. I felt like saying, "It's not the money. It's just—" What? I couldn't think what.

Brent sat there and sat there staring out the window while

the day just pined away. So did I. I don't know what we were waiting for. I was beyond sleep and covered with blood.

Then Brent got up and clumped up the stairs to his room. I was left there with the clock ticking and you could hear the crickets and frogs just starting up for it to be night.

I thought about Janet and if I would ever see her again. She wrote sometimes and I wrote sometimes. But I knew it must be hard for her and she had to get on with her life and two thousand miles is a long way to be from somebody. But you never know. Janet can surprise you. She said she liked me. So you just never know.

Finally, you could hear the bedroom door open and my uncle's footsteps creaking along the wood floor. Then he went and talked with Brent. Aunt Marcie came down to the kitchen and started to cook dinner. I felt embarrassed for her.

After awhile she said with her back to me, "You better clean yourself up."

I went to the pump outside and took off my shirt and my pants and wrung them out under the water. I took my muddy Nikes, watered them down, and left them to dry. Then I pumped a bucketful and poured it over my head. I got as clean as I could and dried myself with Jancy's blanket hanging over her stall in the barn. Some of her horsehairs got stuck in my hair and on my undershirt and underpants.

I went back to the kitchen just like that and went up to my aunt who was washing a dish in the sink and put my arm around her. All I could think of to say was, "I'm sorry."

You could tell she might cry but didn't want to.

"What have you got to be sorry about, young man?" she asked. "Go on upstairs and put some clothes on."

When I was in my bedroom, there was a knock on the door. I opened it and there was Brent with a bunch of clothes in his hands.

"Here," he said, not looking at me.

"Thanks," I said as I took the shirts and pants.

Then he walked away.

It was kind of a somber dinner. Quiet except for night sounds and breathing and the clock ticking and sometimes a truck might go by. I could hardly eat. But my aunt had cooked a good dinner of carrots and mashed potatoes and chicken. She knew it was my favorite.

Sometimes it's funny and I think it was a good thing that Jancy was killed. It's terrible to say that and it tears me up inside. But that's sometimes what I think.

But mostly all I ever wish for is to be walking in the dark on the dirt road hearing the crickets and owls and my feet crunch and smelling the soft wheat air and knowing I'll find Jancy cause she's smart and gentle and wouldn't go far—only to where there's clover special and sweet the way she likes it.

SLAVE TO LOVE

To be that calm. To be that still. To concentrate that intently. I wonder if she is like that all the time. Does her husband love her? Such a complete smile. I have practiced it in my bathroom mirror. But I have a supercilious look that dogs me. It must be the wine. I consulted with an astrologer once who said it was common in people born in my house. Whatever that means. Someone told me I'm too smart to believe in hokum. I believe I'm smart, but I don't think anyone's too smart to believe in hokum.

I don't think I could be a slave to anyone. Even her. She would have to be calm at my conniption fits. Not like I am with Sugar. He pees on the floor, and I say "Bad dog! Go to your room!" Maybe I could learn kindness from her.

I always get her to wait and buy her lottery ticket from me. Twice a week. Always just one. I give it to her with all my luck pouring into the numbers. She never wins. Once, while I was punching the lottery machine, she said she imagines winning for a few seconds after buying. For that, it's worth the dollar, she says. I always wish she'll smile. Sometimes she doesn't, her eyes gentle and her face drawn. I feel pulled into her pain.

One can never predict when she'll come in. If I'm stacking supplies, I may barely get a glimpse of her. But then I rush to the front of the store—with the long-strided gait of those who want to rush but do not wish to show it.

The other clerks know she's my customer. Each of us has favorites. We defer to each other. It is a busy place and it is difficult to keep up with the changing tastes of my colleagues.

Sometimes, too, they wish to serve a customer out of spite, in dead silence tolerating their purchases of beer and chips—putting a can in a small paper bag so they can drink it in their car. How sorry I feel for them. But my colleagues smile and accommodate while cursing them in Vietnamese afterward. They came on a boat off the mainland and sometimes were plucked from the sea shivering deeply to come to America and serve these burly machinists and construction workers their evenings of freedom.

After a few months, I started asking her questions. One question per transaction. She is an engineer. My first image was of this woman in overalls and cap, long hair streaming, standing on the end platform of a caboose, waving to all the children in cars waiting for the train to pass. Or looking up to a bridge and raising her cap to a lady whose toddler was hanging on to the railing, thrilled at the power of the machine that passed beneath him. But these are images from my childhood and my naiveté.

In this town of course she's something oil and gas related. I myself am an MD, but I keep this to myself. I could practice in Pakistan, but I have not bothered to certify myself here.

When my sister came to college here and married an American, then I flocked after her, leaving a meager practice as an internist specializing in the most impecunious of patients. My salary at the store is still about half what I earned there.

My mother couldn't understand why I didn't marry. When I told her Pakistan does not recognize same-sex weddings, she cried. But only once. Then she began teaching me embroidery and cake-making—things my sister disdained. And she taught me a sort of haughty meekness that is the soul, she said, of Pakistani womanhood. She gave me flowers on my birthday, and I hugged her like a woman.

She died shortly after my sister left. My sister could not abide the pain, so I was left to hold my mother's hand. More than that, even, as her physician.

I brought her a garland of orchids, but it did not bring her luck. She was tired of life and did not wish to move to America away from her cool, neat home, radiant with white walls and ceilings, that caught the light in a way no home I've ever seen could imitate.

I live in a small apartment here. I inherited my mother's antiques and linen. My sister could not understand why. She is slow on the uptake, as they say here.

I met a woman in Alabama, which was my first home here. She was dark and small like my mother. She did not wear the shalwar kameez. I did not care. She had short hair and no breasts. I imagined she was a boy.

But she got pregnant. She was sacred then. She could not understand why I barely touched her. I told her I did not wish to stain with my habits the young life growing in her—with my fits of conniption, with my melancholy glasses of wine, with my love of all moods of the moon.

I stayed while she gave birth to my daughter. After, I had to go or I would be crying all the time. I don't know why.

I sold some of the antiques and made a fund for my daughter so that when she grows to be an age when she would like to become an engineer or some such thing that there would be some money waiting for her. I send money every month, too, in cards that smell of lavender. And sometimes I see her and am astounded.

She does not know I am her father, since her mother has married. Her mother has no children by this man. And she is pleased with her girl. I am glad the girl is really a girl and not like me, who cannot make up his mind, although whose body seems to jump to conclusions far sooner than he would have liked.

It is seven years since I have had sex. I went on a spree with wine and young men after my daughter was born. I was thirty then, but I had inherited my mother's oldness. It was unpleasant to slow down after sharing a bottle of pungent red wine and cry that life carried me on a strange sea voyage. As though it was stranger than what these boys would tell me. Some of them would come to me bleeding. They would be grateful and say I had gentle hands. But I never gave money, so rarely would I see one long.

Sari, the engineer, came in today and asked me to a gathering at her home. I accepted. Maybe I can see for certain if her husband is attentive. I rather think he is, but I imagine he is not. I am not certain she understands her effect. I think if she did she would not come into the store to torture my imagination.

I go a few blocks from the store to a home filled with brightness and color and know deep in my bowels that they are loving with each other. There is a crowd of all the people they meet in their lives to whom they wish to give thanks: clerks and waiters and cooks and salespeople.

The food is simple and in very good taste. I eat one of everything. I drink their wine. It is particularly intoxicating. I know it will bring on a fit of melancholy. But luckily I have eaten more than my stomach can bear, and I have to excuse myself to the bathroom. It smells of rosemary, and I am sick to my stomach.

I come out and stare at their backyard. I cannot resist saying to Sari: "My life grows like your grass, lush and green and full of promise. But not constrained like yours. I am full of weeds."

She turns her head to one side and reaches out her hand to hold mine. Just for a second. I can barely stop the tears. It is like holding my mother's hand.

It is true. I cannot call up the demons of hope. I am left melancholy even though my stomach is empty. Everyone I have loved is attached—even to death.

But I will find another and another to fill my heart until I die. I have neglected to learn the art of commingling my life with another's. And so I feel the pain of neglect. Maybe someday I shall learn to overcome my blundering silence and love someone who can love me back. Then I shall be closer to death and it will not matter.

BEHIND THE SCENES

"**W**hat do you miss most in Joshua?" This was the question lingering in the room filled with reporters and photographers. "His presence?" "His body?"

"*Sex?*" The word they were after.

Instead, she said, "I miss everything about him."

She had her wish, though, that he would die in her arms. No lingering. But she was dismayed that her blooming health would likely keep her here for many years essentially alone on this strange planet.

Her influence was strong upon a close inner circle but, despite her radiant fame, negligible in the wider world.

There were only so many superstars and they did not form a club devoted to curing the world of its savage fits. Instead, they transported people from it, no matter how serious the entertainment. She did not star in "serious" films anyway. She had been known as a dark beauty—a dark horse that always won, year after decade after half-century.

Joshua had kept her centered on her human life, not the giga-pixeled images sprawled on billboards since she could remember almost. He had designed her gowns, noted for their grace, their flowing satins, their simplicity. They had been to many parties, but always quietly left at ten.

So she went home from the press conference today, a quick escape in a car no one would look for. Her daughter stayed with her during the funeral and will-reading. Angela was the executrix anyway. There was little to say, some taxes to pay, and the fuss was over. She told Angela she would rather be alone. It was not true, but she was an actress, so she made it sound true.

She talked to friends over the phone. Many asked if they could come by, but again she said she'd rather be alone. These people would not understand why she had to walk into Josh's closet and stare at his jackets and pants, so solemn and flat. Or why she wore her Oscar gown for the next three days, complete with a spray of orchids she had delivered as if from her lover, waiting on the sofa for him to arrive from his store to escort her to her evening of glory.

They had never married because she wished forever to refer to him as her lover.

She slipped under the bedcovers and reached out next to her. Gone was his immediacy, his brown-eyed glance, his sense of fitness, if one could say that in all seriousness about a tailor.

She did not wish to die yet. But she hated this indignity of death that left one longing for the other. The poignancy that makes trees so stoic, branching headlong to the light in all weathers. No, no. It was what they had wanted her to say. It was the sex. If they had asked her now, that's what she would answer.

She would go to a sex store, that's what she'd do. Maybe she'd find something: a robot, a beating heart, something phallic.

"Yes," Josh would say. "Now maybe the time is right."

So she looked on her computer and found some likely places— some open twenty-four hours, maybe for hookers who might need an implement the way homebuilders needed nails or hammers or a piece of pipe.

She got in the car and drove. It was midnight. The store was huge and lighted like noon. She got a cart. Wheeled it along a whole aisle of dildos. A dozen shelves of condoms. Contraptions she did not linger to learn about.

A few others ambled about. None looked embarrassed, just preoccupied. Normally, Josh would have had her home to bed. They would have faced each other and clasped the last clasp of the day.

A friend of hers had told her not to try a vibrator or she'd never prefer the real thing again. She saw all the different sizes and sorts and commanded herself to seem interested. It was a gift for a friend. It was for her daughter. It was to complement a sculpture she had on the mantelpiece.

All she could think of to say to the checkout person was, "My lover died."

But she said nothing.

The clerk looked right into her eyes. "Paper or plastic?"

She opened her package at home and examined the fake phallus. Would it not be better to take up with some young man who could bear her slow kisses and bony bottom if money were on the bedside table? This was not all there was to love, surely, all these animal years.

It felt uncannily real. She sat on the bed and inserted the batteries. She would turn down the lights. She would be all ready, just as with Joshua.

She lay under the covers and clasped the phallus to her belly. She could not do this.

She turned it on and it vibrated against her breast. She closed her eyes and longed for it to kiss her, to caress her.

She could not put it inside her. Its magic could not conjure up anything more than what it was. This was it: The indignity of death. Sad. Lonely. Ludicrous.

But she could not keep this device in her home. When she died, she did not want it found among her things. People might think that is how old people did it. People might think Joshua was not a full lover to her or that her responses had been lukewarm. So she drove back to the store at three in the morning.

"We don't do takebacks," said the same young clerk.

"There is no substitute," she said. She looked the man full in the face.

"That is the first real excuse I've heard," he seemed to say with his silence as he looked back at her, without hesitation refunding her money.

As she rode back in the darkness, it rained.

After reaching her driveway, she sat in her car till the wet night subsided and the first sun touched her roses. She slid out and smelled their soft yellow petals. The sky was streaked with the silent pink clouds of the coming day.

THE ARRANGEMENT

I am alive.

Even though I live in a large city, I can see the vast and gracious sky. Its blueness—especially in winter on a crisp day—is perfect, even though I know its hue is simply a fluke. White and gray clouds drift in shapes that defy description—peaked, rounded, streaked, wisped. Billions of tons, yet buoyed as steel planes, fueled without fuel and impossible to walk upon. I look up often and seek the sun, which, though just a tiny star, brings beloved light. Even the most overcast sky cannot stop its rays. Instead, the grass and palm trees, the black, orange, brown, and windowed shops are darker and as saturated at noon as at sunset.

I see the contours of the natural world—the patches of tufted lawn, live oaks overarching lazy boulevards. I hear grackles, sparrows, and mockingbirds, and watch dragonflies dart amongst the cars and trucks, then up and up twice and thrice above the traffic lights. I see the travel of the sun from winter southwest to summer northwest as the shadow of my blinds on the floor wanders with the months. I see the colors of the deciduous trees change, slowly, from late fall through late winter: yellow, ripe orange, deep red. A lone autumn-red tree in the midst of January is a lovely secret revealed, next to the burgeoning tulip trees bursting with the beginning of a long and sweet spring.

I am telling you this out of compassion—I hope, at any rate, it is compassion—for the very being I am, born into a confusion of love and care, fierce tensions and alcohol, talent and broken crockery.

But, here, I have a story to tell, and this is all to set the scene.

* * *

My brother Simon lived in a big house in West University. His room was small, with a small single bed made up with sheets depicting giraffes and lions, and a bedspread of monkeys and parrots.

A mobile hung from the ceiling close to the window. It cascaded in oblong shapes of red, blue, and yellow, with indentations in them, like artists' palettes. In the soft currents of the air, the mobile gently and slowly twirled and rocked.

Simon spent hours a day watching it—the way the light from the window changed the deepness of its colors, the way the shadows trickled and careened over the wall. Soundless and ever-moving, the mobile was Simon's impetus to think—to think deeply of life's despairs and beauties, of the people he knew yet who scarcely knew him because of his shyness and eventual irritation at having to speak at all.

Simon worked at a flower shop. He had an eye for beauty and could create arrangements his employers knew were far and away more beautiful than those learned in classes. They decided Simon should not know how good he was, or he would ask for more money or leave for a better position.

These people, the Witislowskis, were from Stanislawow, Poland. They had lived during World War II as Jews under Hitler. Acacia, the wife—renamed in America, as was her husband, Jude —clung to the fortune they made at their shop, hoping for great things from their only child, Rebecca.

They had been chosen at whim as unwilling functionaries answerable to the Nazis and had helped herd their fellow citizens into a ghetto specially created from the poorest district of town, then further herded them to the Jewish cemetery where eight thousand one day were shot or smothered in huge graves they had been made to dig the day before. The twenty-seven thousand remaining Jews died slowly over the next five years of malnutrition, infectious diseases, injuries, wounds, gunshot, pure exhaustion, and overwhelming depression.

It was this sort of thing, thought Simon, that people did not know about the Holocaust: It was not just in concentration camps that good and generous, ordinary and extraordinary people died, but whole towns carried on fitful, slow pogroms during those five long years.

A special road, built by his neighbors under Jude's direction, carried the dead from the ghetto in rickety carts right out of the nineteenth century and dumped them into further mass graves, where the bodies were doused in lime.

Jude had a fragment of parchment, once part of a Torah, kept on his desk as a reminder that he and his wife had survived. It was terrible what they had seen, what they had been forced to do, they said. They had never known when they might be killed, too. But they were here as God's witnesses to these dreadful events. Their hearts were pure.

In addition to his bed, mobile, and window, Simon had a large bookcase filled with paperbacks—philosophy and literature, ancient and modern from all cultures—whose well-split spines spoke to his familiarity with their contents.

He had a small desk and chair, where he wrote every day in a notebook, even if it were only one sentence, such as: "The ostrich does indeed bury its head in the sand, but there is at least sand in which he can bury it." Sometimes his observations carried on to a few words more: "It is trite today to say God is made in man's image, but I think it is the quality and strength of that image, in addition to the inclusion of a vastness beyond even an astrophysicist's imagining, beyond and beyond and deep, with a depth that the sharp conciseness of a black hole only begins to reflect, that makes a conception of the Eternal ring with the clarity of immense obliqueness."

He wrote slowly, contemplating his words as a painter would the shadow made of obstructions to the sun on his lover's face.

He read his books slowly, too, every evening, noting cryptic words that struck him roundly. Sometimes he would read a paragraph ten times. When he finished a book, one could say he had read it fully.

Simon had not graduated high school. Yet by the time he was twenty-eight, he found he could enroll in a college after taking an IQ test, and no one cared he hadn't studied the subjunctive mood in French or that he had the barest concept of the calculus.

He was troubled by the world he saw and sought in study —whether on his own or at the university—a way to try to get a handle on how humankind had managed, with such good potential, to keep getting itself into such messes. He in particular wondered why he had been born, since his mother had stated many times when he was young that he had been a "mistake."

"I am a mistake," he thought. "Yet I am as alive as my sister. Does she feel better because she is wanted? I don't know. She took cocaine, stole money, spent time in jail, and sees a psychiatrist. I do not think she feels wanted. I don't know how to ask her."

He could not understand how his very life was the result of his mother not using a diaphragm when his father had been in her vagina. It troubled him that he could never find an apartment he could pay for. He had tried three times, and had always come back to the room at his father's house. He could not get rid of his feeling of debasement. He felt like the man who had become a cockroach—only he had felt like a cockroach for as long as he could remember.

From time to time, he played lacrosse with some of his high-school friends. He was good. Muscular and fast. And liked a couple of beers once he'd had a strenuous game.

He rarely saw his Dad, even though most of the time Simon lived in his house, but with a separate entrance to his little room. He hung his head, and his stomach squelched at the thought of begging, but sometimes he knocked on his father's door, greeting him with a hug. He knew Joseph knew that he really wanted a beer or two, and tried to make Simon feel independent yet at home.

When Simon was in college, at the age of thirty, he became close friends with a Catholic girl in her early twenties. Colleen had brilliant auburn hair close-plaited into two braids that descended slightly beyond her waist. Her skin, her open face, was pale, lacking the freckles that usually accompanied reddish hair. She had floral green eyes that crinkled with love for her boyfriend. She felt enriched at having such a worldly and learned man, eight years her senior, to help her navigate the crusty world of philosophy.

But they disagreed about God. When he undid her braids as she sat on his tiny bed with the childish bedclothes, she ignored everything but his books and his shimmering mobile and deft hands.

"Ah," he said, "I have been longing to do this ever since I met you."

She blushed.

"Your beauty astounds me," he said.

He took her hair in his fingers and wrapped its tendrils round her breasts, feeling both with a tenderness she had not thought possible in a man.

"May I see you naked?" he asked.

She looked away, blushing even more deeply, and nodded.

She lifted her t-shirt over her head, exposing her simple brassiere. They looked shyly into each other's eyes. Hesitantly, he unhooked the rounded garment and let it fall.

"You're perfect," he said. "You're why I exist."

She looked at him, puzzled by the enormity he made of her body.

"I am far from perfect," she said. "I am lost. But you help me understand."

"You, lost?" he said, puzzled by the enormity she made of his knowledge. "I know so little. I understand so little. You understand as naturally as a hummingbird hovers its beak into nectar."

They made love slowly and tenderly, as he studied her body and seemed to extract an ecstasy from every move she made. He knew it was her first time and he didn't want the scorching fuck he had had with a drunken chicken farmer's wife when he was nineteen. It had forever scorched his mind, as had his mother's blows when he was three.

Afterward, she asked him the one question he dreaded, knowing she attended Mass every Sunday and confession every month. "Do you believe in God the Father, God the Son, and God the Holy Ghost?"

"Acchh," he said. "And what does it matter if I do or I don't? I am alive and I am happy now, and you, you seem happy, too."

"But I have broken a promise I made to my parents."

"Oh," he said. "Shouldn't you have said so earlier? It would not have mattered. Viewing your body is all I would have needed."

"I am sorry. Under her breath when I was twelve, I heard my mother say she never refused my father, but she never liked it."

"Oh," he said again.

He was silent for a moment.

"Did you like it?"

"Yes, oh yes!" she cried. "You know me so well. You are a real lover."

"Yes," he said. "Real. A real lover."

"But God."

"Yes," he said. "But God."

They lay close together on the tiny bed, the linen with lions and parrots sporadically covering their bodies.

"You are a great man," she said with simple certitude.

"Aacch, no," he replied. "I try to grasp a speck of the universe and am constantly failing."

He pointed to his mobile.

"Just look at that—its perfection, its invention. My father could explain it with physics. But to me it is something beyond comprehension. It is a wonder that such a thing came from such wild beasts as we."

"I think," she said tentatively, "I think you have little idea of your own beauty."

"*My* beauty," he said as he sat up quickly. "I have no beauty. Only restlessness. And a profound lack of understanding how to get money enough for my wants without damning my conscience."

"But people need some form of money to live," she said. "Life is not free."

"Well, yes, it is," he countered. "It's free. Then you reach an age where all you can do is work on a chicken farm because your parents have entered the cage of a lion who will rip them to bits, yet still he kills it with a gun. And they leave with its blood on their hands and turn their backs on each other, while they grieve over the loss of the lion—though it would have killed them both."

They were silent. Simon slid over Colleen and dressed, hiding the slim and muscular, nearly hairless body it had been his pleasure to share with her.

"You must go now," he said. "I must study. I have intruded enough into your life and made you do something you promised not to do."

"It's not your fault," she protested, trying to grasp his hand like a supplication. He returned with a warm clasp.

"It *is* my fault," he said slowly, head bowed. "Religion—especially Christianity—does not touch me the way it does you. To me it is pagan and cannibalistic. To you it is glowing candles and devotion and a sacrifice of self you don't even think about."

She lay there, unable to move. There was a red spot on the sheet and a few streaks of blood on her thighs.

"I love you," she said. "You are deep."

They were both quiet as he moved to his desk and opened a book.

"Must I choose?" she asked.

He read a bit, then stopped and folded his book, slipping his pen into it to hold his place.

"We cannot go far," he said. "It is not so much a choice as it is whether you think it worthy to embrace human knowledge and set aside those things which, while enlightening for awhile, stale in the face of eternity."

"I do not think I can do that. When I confess my soul, I am cleansed. When I take the sacraments, I am freed of my sins."

"Just so," he said.

"Then," he said rather more stiffly, "what of all this?"

He gestured to his floor-length bookcase. "There are other books to study and other people to learn from."

"But the tradition. The connection with the past."

"I think the Bible is a wonderful book. It is replete with fascinating stories, philosophy, moral seeking, and the wonderment of the love we can grow to have for our fellow humans and other life on Earth."

"Then why...?"

"It is not the only nor even the most important book. In fact, there is no 'more important' book. Just some that are more influential and meaningful than others. And certainly the Bible is one of those."

So they remained friends for his remaining years at college. They never discussed anything but the books they were studying. They never made love again.

When she graduated, Simon gave her a small crystal crucifix to wear around her neck. She was touched and puzzled. She then got a job as a buyer in women's clothing at a department store and moved to New York. Her mother evidently had not only connections but also ambitions for her daughter.

Simon didn't finish college. He was two courses short when Colleen graduated. He suddenly felt deflated and his room seemed sparse. He found an opening at a flower shop.

"Why not steep myself in beauty?" he asked himself. "Though I know so little of it."

And thus he came to Acacia's and Jude's shop. He knew little about them but Jude's grotesque task during the war. Acacia told him that when they'd arrived in America, they had managed to lead a respectable and violence-free life in the midst of the countryside, tending to chickens.

Why, thought Simon, was it always chicken farmers he ran into? He got his first job through a school friend whose uncle owned a farm. The smell of shit was egregious, the sound of the clucking hens was meaningless, the quarters they lived in were impossibly cramped, and the eggs they laid never stopped coming

—though he loved the delicacy of the brown and white eggs, feeling their fragile bumps as his hands clasped gently round them.

He slid into his adult life with as slippery a move as his first amidst the crap that covered that clucking floor. He worked there four years, with no hope of promotion. It was a family business, and the sullen son, Mark, never stopped reminding him that *he* was Simon's boss and that would always be the case. Not, thought Simon, the most diplomatic way to keep employees for the long term.

So Simon quit, with a little nest egg, so to speak, returned to Houston, and lived quietly in a small, roach-infested apartment for another four years, immersed in his writing and his books and independent of his father except for the odd beer or two after a lacrosse game.

All he wanted was to study and write notes in his spiral books. Why were there not garrets now like those Balzac had paid a few sous for—that it was expected for young writers to live in while they germinated their genius? But he was greatly discouraged, for although bits of his writing impressed him, most of it was garbage not fit to meet a publisher's eye. He felt like a turd in the bowels of God—even though a devout agnostic.

Then the money ran out.

He turned to his father, who, while expecting him to find a responsible position, welcomed him into his home. The room was available, after all, and had space for all his possessions.

"A responsible position." This phrase puzzled Simon. What did "responsible" mean? A butcher was responsible for cutting up meat. He could not stand the sight of dead animals, so he did not want to be responsible for doing something like that. A Wall Street trader made money every time he traded stocks for a client. Was this a responsible way to make money? It made investing in companies a good thing, provided a measure of liquidity to the company, and gave it some standing relative to other companies. It made some sense of businesses that had to be big and had to have a lot of money because there were so many customers to cater to. There were too many people in the world, he thought. And this stocks and bonds business was one way to finance all that consumption. But it depressed Simon, and he could find no purpose in simply manipulating money.

Simon had read there were great advances in the landfill business and that most garbage could be crushed to an unrecognizable size compared to its original bulkiness. He applied to companies that picked up and disposed of the city's garbage.

After undergoing training, he worked as the "schlepper," the lowest-paid job in the business. He wheeled the plastic garbage containers to the back of the truck and tipped them in or simply hauled the bags and slung them in. He enjoyed the physicality of his work.

He stayed at his father's house until he was twenty-eight, when he discovered he could enter college without having finished high school.

He lived frugally and had saved up enough to pay for his courses, but not for his books or food. By then, he owned a ten-year-old Corolla for whose gas he had an arrangement with a local gas station that operated a garage: Every week, he would perform a few oil and lube jobs, for which he had a deft knack, in exchange for gas and minor work on his own car. He would have to confront his father with his lack of schooling. There would be awkward words and a convoluted form of punishment for his having to sponge off him.

Maybe he should ask his sister. But he and she had hardly communicated for years. They had little knowledge of each other's lives. She was older than he and had by then attended college and married well. He guessed all that psychiatric help had worked and she was over any mess in the family—she probably didn't obsess about fine philosophical points the way he did. He looked down on her, yet feared her because she seemed so robust.

And so he had the awkward conversation with his father. On the one hand, his father was delighted he wanted to go to college—and easily forgave him for not having finished high school.

"However," he said, "Once you enter college, you should finish and think about what you want to do with your career."

My career, Simon had thought with vagueness and astonishment. *My career.*

His father was equally delighted that Simon had enough money to cover his tuition.

"I am sorry you cannot study at Rice," he said. "That would be the best place."

And all the intervening years of the chicken farm, his own studies, the garbage trucks, and moving back with his father came down on him, stifling him like a bell jar crafted of shame. He was not living up to his potential. But, then, he had no idea what his potential was. Just a vague notion he wanted to write. There were a few modern writers he admired, but only partially and only with circumspection. Those whose philosophies were hard-won—those he admired. Those whose writing burned with the passionate love of an unbreakable morality and did not become glib as they wrote past their first few sentences.

And so he studied. And so he became aware that most philosophy professors did not burn with the passionate love of an unbreakable morality—but for the few who did, he was grateful and wrote his best essays. He spoke up sometimes. But only in the classes of those he felt an affinity for. But then he felt ashamed at the assumption he could feel affinity for such eminently learned people, while he was only self-taught and an undergrad at that. These people had written books—often good and logical books, he came to find out. He felt hopelessly out of his depth and again like a cockroach, though he tried to pass for a keen student.

Then there was Colleen. Over the years he had had a few affairs. When he splurged by going to a bar for a beer, he sometimes met an interesting woman. These affairs had inevitably gone awry because of the woman's eventual pettiness— though in all ways perfect as all beautiful women were perfect— seeing, for example, the speck of dirt on his shirt, while she missed that he had just bought it to show himself off in a good light to others while with her.

Colleen was different, though. She was deep. But it was a depth of religion that, as he had said, could not touch him. It shut his being out, yet she did indeed engage his mind when they stuck to what they were reading.

He even went with Colleen to Mass once and watched as the ceremony progressed. He watched her downcast face as she emerged having taken the sacraments. It was a deep thing for her—and he could see she wholeheartedly believed Jesus was nourishing her being. He suddenly felt a coldness in his belly, like a loss. But he could not will himself to believe in something he found hopelessly arcane. He felt sorry then that he could not, for he knew he loved Colleen as he would love no other woman.

But then he defied his father and did not finish his degree. He had no idea yet what a career meant. He wanted simply to study and write and discover what he could in his own desultory fashion. He did not want to be burdened with other work that did not speak to his being. Why? What would he teach? What did he know?

But the very best of his attempts at developing a system of knowledge had come to a halt at uncertainty. One could not get rid of uncertainty. He was amazed at people who could speak about politics or current events or even a rock star or a baseball player with absolute certainty. He remembered facts. But they were like detritus in his mind. They muddled his search for—well, for what he thought was—certainty.

Maybe he was just trying too hard to be like everybody else. He was a stranger. He had not been wanted, so he was a stranger. He could not be certain even of himself and the statements he made—although when he spoke he sounded certain.

He thought, instead, he was pretentious, just like every person who aspired to be an intellectual. But towards his father, Simon felt deep shame, and wished his father had been able to come to his graduation like all the other parents.

Simon did not have anything to do with his mother. She lived in Alabama, married to an auto mechanic. They lived in a little house, with two donkeys, a few goats, and, again, loads of chickens. They had a patch of land from which they grew vegetables, so his mother did not want for food. Both she and her husband made home-distilled whiskey, a passion for which each enjoyed as they knocked each other about in drunken raging.

He observed this latter fact when he had stayed with her for two weeks, when he was on vacation during his garbage days. He thought she was living a good life near the soil, of the Earth, and he had grown to admire that. He had gone to visit in the spirit of forgiveness. But, as he turned his back on her door, walking out with his backpack tugging at his shoulders as she waved at him, he did not look back.

One day, while working at the flower store, Simon came across a tiny book, translated into English from the Hebrew by a man whose first language, it appeared from the lurching, barely paragraphed text, was not English. It was a homey but scrupulous documentary of what had happened to the Jews during the Holocaust in the town where Acacia and Jude had lived.

It was dusty and had obviously been neglected for years at the back of an obscure shelf in the storeroom. Simon read a few sentences, then slipped the tiny book into his pocket. There was more to the story of his employers' war experiences than they had ever let on. He wanted to find out. To have survived the Holocaust—to have faced degrading death during the Holocaust—he regarded as probably the most courageous thing a person in the twentieth century could have done.

When he returned to his father's house that day, the sun and clouds interplayed in the atmosphere in such a way as to produce lovely, smoky streaks and billows, mingled with rose in a vast display across the western sky. This had merged into an orangey hue before the light dissipated into twilight.

He lost himself in the beauty of the sight, wondering as he always did, whether other people noticed such things in a big city—so much ground, so many buildings, so many freeways and roads, so much indoors—or if outdoors, then running or walking with head facing blindly ahead, focusing so much on muscle that the sun—that made Earth possible and without which muscle was so much nothing—became a nuisance that made seeing difficult. But, no, to him he could not think it was difficult to look at the sun at sunset, for then it was soft and bearable upon the eyes.

Simon wanted to read the little book. He did not want to return to the flower shop without having read every page. He wanted to know what had happened to Stanislawow, he wanted to know if the Witislowskis were mentioned. He wanted to know what had become of any children besides Rebecca.

Rebecca was forty-five, never married, and quietly lived her life selling CDs at a family-run disc store. It also served as a lending library. They had a listening room. And Rebecca took advantage at every lunch hour to listen to what was supposed to be the greatest music the world had to offer—expanding her musical universe with what she formerly viewed as ineluctably foreign and scarifying sounds.

She had many friends. She had attended college and earned an undergraduate degree in psychology, with a view towards becoming a psychotherapist. But understanding people was difficult for her. One that involved much study and many sleepless hours. She had concluded she simply was not a passionate woman. She was a friend, she loved passionate music. But she could not love another human being. She did not have feelings like them and therefore would not be able to respond to them in a well-thought-through, therapeutic manner.

She did not even have feelings for her parents. She respected them, but left home as soon as possible and eluded their grasp upon her future, turning down dates they would arrange for her with "eligible" bachelors.

At heart she knew she did not trust her parents. They acted with duty but without sincerity. They hired talented employees, for example, but did not reward them with praise or anything but the barest minimum of raises. They relied on their employees' skills and scoured the schools for the best, as-yet-unidentified talent. They had a bookkeeper, Christina, who assiduously performed all her duties and willingly worked for the Witislowskis for years. Christina was profoundly unassuming and did not seem to appreciate the immense value she provided for her employers.

The Witislowskis, with the help of their backroom apprentice, arranged all the buying—which was the fun part of the job. But it was their backroom apprentice—now Simon—who performed with all the panache of a professional and produced results that made the Witislowskis well-to-do.

Even Rebecca, thought Simon, as he leafed through the tiny book, even she did not know its contents. Of this he was sure.

He read about Stanislawow's massacre, in one day, of eight thousand Jews out of its seventy thousand inhabitants, of the twenty-seven thousand who were left, and how the poorest part of town was evacuated and the twenty-seven thousand Jews were made to squash themselves into tiny, dirty rooms. How there were too many Jews to fit in that area, and how those who didn't fit, too, were massacred. How the intelligentsia were attacked first—the physicians and professors—so there were few to lead or heal the starving Jewish population.

Names were mentioned here and there, but it was not until he reached page forty-five that the name Witislowski came up. It seemed that there was a young man who had just finished dental school. He was Polish—not Jewish—and the Nazis discovered he was excellent at making caps. Gold was not scarce, as the Nazis had taken all the Jews' belongings, so there were many gold bracelets and rings from which to make caps. Witislowski took over the equipment of a Jew who had been shot into the mass grave with the eight thousand.

Simon could not believe what he was reading. He had accepted his lot with them, loving the flowers, and bemusedly performing his creative arrangements—accepting it, as he thought, in a manner that Mendel had accepted his lot in growing and noting generations of pea plants, silent and mostly alone. Simon had notebooks filled with each of the arrangements he had devised—complete with tiny sketches—so he could build an old one from four or five years ago, and no one would recognize it was not new.

According to the book, Dr. Witislowski had saved up enough money to marry the daughter of one of the Nazi officials. He had fallen in love with her at one of many dinners he enjoyed with one Nazi family in particular.

She had been there throughout the destruction of the town's Jewish homes and synagogues. She had been a witness to the slaughter of the eight thousand—later to weekly shootings of five hundred as the Jewish population shrank in cold and filth, morbid life, and fear. She had visited the ghetto many times, a sour-faced Aryan in Mrs. Muransky's black fur coat, delivering black peasant bread to be issued in tiny quantities each day to each Jew. She had picked up a little Polish. Enough to fool Simon. Enough to fool the French, in whose country she and the dentist ended up after eloping from the city.

They were a compromised pair. What they had done and what they had seen were devastating. They disassociated, Simon thought. They thought only of themselves—then of each other—and no one else mattered. And that, he concluded, was how they lived their lives. He faced the fact once and for all that he was wasted in their employ.

"Career!" Sure. *Career.*

He wanted now to do only one thing: To ruin their lives—not to the extent they had seen other lives ruined and destroyed. But to get to them—inside their beings. Not by any illegal or nefarious means, but nonetheless to get to them.

Simon stared at his mobile. He felt the full effect of the moral morass into which he had unwittingly stepped. He was thirty-eight. He lived with his father. He slept in a single bed meant for a child. He was obsessed with moral certitude and a peaceful resolution to his wrestle with a God that was so vast and so unknowable he always felt defeated. He still played lacrosse with his two loyal high school friends—one of whom had tested positive for HIV yet still was remarkably healthy—and their circle of friends. He was physically strong, yet unutterably shy, still bearing others' company rarely—each time was a great event for him.

First, he knew he must meet with Rebecca. She must know about her parents. He was recklessly certain in a way he was certain about snatching a lacrosse ball. He was an aggressive player on the field in a way that puzzled his friends, yet accepted with enthusiasm.

Once Simon had made up his mind, he did not think. He simply called her and said he had news about her parents she ought to know.

"I know about my parents," she said. "So I am not surprised you do, too."

"How do you mean, 'know'?" he asked.

"How absolutely selfish and grubbing they are," she continued.

How involuted they were, wanting only a big house and a big car and a swimming pool and a great match for their daughter. She knew they were profoundly disappointed in her. They could sense she had cottoned on to them at an early age and had grown to dislike her for seemingly taking the moral high ground.

"No," Simon said. "That is not what I mean. Although it is, really, what I mean."

And he then said he needed to talk to her face-to-face to tell her the true story and show her the evidence.

Rebecca was wary of strangers, and, although Simon was a known quantity to her, she still knew him very little—or so she thought. She did not want to meet him either at her place or his.

They met at a coffee shop. Simon was immediately struck by her gentleness and awkwardness as she apologized for not meeting at her place.

"I just thought, you know," she stumbled, "a more neutral ground."

"I understand," he said. "This is news of a shocking nature and you would expect to have some privacy later on to express whatever it is you need to express."

What right had he to deepen the rift—perhaps beyond repair—between her and her parents? Would it not be better for him to just leave now, say he was wrong, he had been mistaken?

But he had piqued her conscience. There was something morally scurrilous her parents had done. He sensed she was the type of person who must know. She had already shown disinterest in inheriting her parents' money, as the bookkeeper had confided in him. She had rejected nine suitors, seeing the dollar signs shining in their eyes. She had many friends, none of whom she invited to meet her parents. Her parents had very few friends—mostly Polish, and mostly made from the same fabric as they—or so she thought.

He brought the little book out of his pocket and put it in her hand, placing his other hand over the book as she held it, wondering.

"On page forty-five you will find the start of the story of your parents," he said. "But read it from the beginning. It is not easy to read—the English is bad, but the events described are far, far worse."

He told her how he had come across the book and how it was her road to discovering who her parents really were. This, he thought, was something she seemed to want to know.

"You wanted to be a psychologist," he ventured.

"A psychotherapist."

"Ah. Well, I think knowing your past is somehow a prerequisite to being in that field, is it not?"

"Yes. We ourselves go to therapists and discover ourselves. I just never thought there was much to discover. I am so boring."

"You are a friend to so many."

"I bore myself. So I listen to others. They confide in me. They know they can trust me to keep a confidence."

"So, well, trust me to keep *your* confidence."

She said she would, and left without drinking her coffee. Simon slowly ate a bagel, thinking its association somehow with Jewishness was a vague and simple homage to the act he had just performed. The greatest act of interference in his life.

It was almost closing time when Simon finally left the coffee shop. He walked along the darkened street to where he'd parked his car. When he turned on the ignition, Schubert's

"Arpeggione" Sonata was just starting, fitting into his life as though he had chosen it himself. Listening from its very first note, he drove slowly home, until its last note, as he waited in his father's garage.

He noticed the living room lights were still on. He wanted desperately to talk to his father, but he did not know what to say. What had he done? Rebecca lived alone. She had embraced Judaism with the certitude she was a Jew, and had many friends to share holy days and festivals with. How would she react when she discovered she was not really Jewish? How did she really feel about her parents? Were her illusions so stripped from her that this would simply be further confirmation? People were strange about their parents. They could murder and embezzle, yet still people ran to them with love and forgiveness.

He had been thus prepared with his own mother. His father simply was all physics. That was all that mattered to him: Order out of chaos. Joseph did not focus on uncertainty —though Heisenberg had discerned it. One could find certainty in physics—not the mystical deepening awareness of the eternal and the mysterious that had so affected Einstein—if one rigidified one's being, as Simon perceived his father had. Simon did not seek certainty in rigidity but rather in some essence that was unquantifiable.

No, he would look at his mobile and contemplate beauty, hoping all the while that Rebecca would take the knowledge well. If not, he was responsible. He would make amends. He would find a way to make amends.

Many days passed, and Rebecca did not call.

Acacia and Jude were the official florists to many synagogues, each of which had a different floral arrangement under the bima every Shabbat. These were the showpieces of their business, from which much other business flowed. They advertised in the Jewish newspaper.

One Friday morning, when he was busy preparing such an arrangement, Rebecca stepped into the back room. She had bypassed meeting her parents.

She looked at peace. Simon was momentarily relieved, then dispirited by her sudden vehemence.

"I am the child of the worst of liars and cheaters and conmen and bystanders to evil, panderers to evil," she blurted.

"You must keep the book," she said as she pushed it into his hands.

How could he tell her? His parents had many moral dilemmas they faced with sluggish abandonment and denial. It was not just the Holocaust. It was every human being who had to learn how to be, dare he say it in just plain terms, "decent"?

He was a philosopher, he explained. Not a very good one. I cannot teach anyone anything. And I hardly know what I have learned, he explained.

"Please, sit down. Please," he pleaded.

She would not. She just stood there. "I cannot work. I cannot believe my father could shape a tooth from the gold of a Jew's wedding ring and place it in a Nazi's mouth so he could eat better, while the whole town's Jewish population—all but barely a handful—dwindled with starvation, cold, and bestial murder."

She explained that her father had bought a dentist's chair and a bit of equipment and performed simple operations for friends. He did not have the requisite American certification, so it was always done on the sly. This was proof enough these were her parents the book talked about.

Rebecca said she had been about to hang herself, when her telephone rang.

She had picked it up and heard her father's voice. She could not say anything more than the initial, "Hello."

Her father had slammed down the receiver, yelling at his daughter's insolent silence. Insolent! It was impossible to confront him. He had married a Nazi's daughter. She knew her mother kept in touch with her father—that he was still alive in his nineties in Germany, untouched by investigations following the war, blending, as a native who avoided his former acquaintances, into the population as a good German—who, as Rebecca thought, had escaped from Poland as a Jew after the war.

How could she live with such knowledge? She had one gold cap in her mouth herself, which her father had installed. Did he have a cache of Jewish gold still? She wouldn't eat on that side of her mouth. Then she made an appointment with her prosthodontist and had him remove the gold cap and replace it with porcelain.

Simon was relieved to hear of this one positive step.

"My parents will return any minute," she said, "and I have no desire to see them."

What was he to do? He could not fathom life. He had been unwanted. But now maybe there was a way he was wanted. He knew what she felt like—or thought he did—as though if she saw them she would run out of the shop and under the wheels of a speeding car. She felt false—like an odd carbuncle on the skin of her parents' diseased lives.

People have to survive, he thought. But there is a limit, and there are things you do not do. Or if you did, then you talked about them—especially if your daughter is now forty-five—you expressed sorrow, guilt—something more than fabricating a story of duty and stoicism and escape from oppression.

"Will you marry me?" he blurted.

He had no idea that was what he would say. But now he knew his purpose.

"Will you marry me?" he said again, softly, and took her hand in his.

*   *   *

In spite of my brother's assumptions, it has taken me five decades to build the mind I thought I'd lost. My brother also almost lost his mind. I think he would have hanged himself, too, had Rebecca done the same.

We are not estranged as once we were—the one "wanted," the other not. He has always lived his life courageously, though on the edge. And this courage to face his own self-loathing helped him be the pillow on which his wife could lie and face her life without drowning in it.

51

SMOKE AND FIRE

She loved the deep rush of smoke-filled air dragging to the bottom of her lungs. Then holding her breath a moment and letting it seep out her mouth and nose slowly—patterns of blue-gray mist floating, twisting, then dissipating.

Smoking in the dark was anathema to her. She had to see the charred air wisping through the transparent atmosphere. There was nothing like it—not watching steam rise from a scorching cup of coffee nor the cold winter air gushing out that hurt breathed in.

She abhorred knowing what she was breathing, though. Her teeth were yellow. The short hairs on her upper lip had turned faintly orange-brown until she waxed them away. The sides of the fingers she used to hold the cigarettes had long been stained. She hated waking up coughing, reaching for the hard cardboard cigarette pack (she did not like how the soft packs squished lightly) and lighting up first thing—the first real breath of the day.

Although she resented the thought, she nonetheless did not want her daughter to see her smoking anymore. So she was visiting a psychologist.

But to give up even hearing the match strike and pull along the sandpapery edge of the box, smelling and savoring the sight of the brief flame, and that first bright pulled-in breath. Even huddling in the wind and cold outside the house so her daughter could be spared. Most of all, the rush of calm that came with each drag, there an instant, then gone. She envied men their pipes and cigars.

She had stopped dozens of times. The men she had liked were adamant about her quitting. She could not stay quit for any of them.

She explained this to the psychologist.

"Why did you start again?" was the obvious question.

"I don't wish to be owned," she answered, to her surprise. "I don't wish to give in that much."

The therapist was silent.

"You want me to say more?" she asked.

"Do *you* want to?"

"I need a reason."

"You ashamed of smoking?"

"People I've never met have opinions of me."

"Why *this* way to be different?"

"At work I'm in all weathers outdoors with two fat ladies who rattle on and on."

"And you're alone in your private life."

"Except for my daughter."

Again they were silent. She looked at the comfortable man opposite her. She felt angry and wanted to leave.

"I want to be accepted."

"No, you don't. You want to rebel. You're daring someone to like you even though you smoke."

"But you don't understand. It's better than sex."

"Then you've never had good sex."

"You've never smoked."

"I have."

"You don't now."

"Two packs a day. Aggravates my ulcers. I quit a hundred times."

She felt angrier. "Why don't you just smoke a pipe?"

"Smoking's smoking."

She could hardly wait for the session to end.

On the way to her car, she got out a cigarette, lit a match, and took that precious first drag. I've quit for an hour, she thought. Does that count? Bastard. *Quit a hundred times.* Bullshit.

Everyone was against her. It was supposed to be a free society. These so-called professionals think they know everything. She'd seen pictures of cut-open lungs. So what. A hundred and fifty dollars for that?

Her daughter was home. It was quarter to four. She'd thought she'd have a couple of hours of peace. "So, Miranda, you're here for what? To gloat?"

"No."

"That damn doctor called here, didn't he."

"You asked him—."

"I never asked *you*."

"I'm involved."

"No, you're not. You self-righteous little bitch."

"Paul's the best man you've ever met."

"What right does he have to make it a condition?"

"You prefer those things over everything."

Miranda's mother put her purse on the kitchen counter. "I'm sorry."

Miranda asked if she'd filled the prescription.

She'd driven past the pharmacy on her third cigarette.

"Forgot," she lied.

"Why is it," asked Miranda, "that every guy you fall for doesn't smoke?"

"Bad luck."

"You make your own luck."

"What makes you so wise?"

"My whole life here is built around being with you as little as possible so you can smoke."

"Are you threatening with your asthma?"

"I don't do it on purpose."

"All right," said her mother. "Let's go to the pharmacy."

Miranda smiled slightly. "Sure?"

"Sure I'm sure."

At the next session she explained it was purely an act of will to drag herself there.

"Here," she said, taking one half-finished and one unopened pack out of her purse. "And the matches."

He gave them back. "I'm not your garbage can."

"I quit for two days."

"Then you started again?"

He asked about the medication.

"I felt calmer. My head felt clearer."

He asked why she started again.

"I talked to Paul on the phone. He misses me."

"Do you miss him?"

"Smoking's a known quantity."

"Do you believe you can quit?"

"Between you and me, I'm forty and no man's going to turn up who's like Paul."

"Even though he doesn't tolerate your smoking?"

"He's got guts to say so. He'd be attractive to many women."

"Why do you think he likes you?"

"He wants to control me."

"Then he *doesn't* like you."

"I don't know."

"What would happen if you really quit and he said, sorry, it's too late?"

"Nonsmokers make it shameful to smoke."

"Sometimes a little shame is a good thing," said her psychologist.

I hate you, she thought.

Miranda was home early again. Her mother blew up again. Miranda didn't budge. This continued after the following several sessions. But she quit for longer and longer.

"I know how drug addicts must feel," she said. "You have to tie them down and let them sweat it out."

"You *are* a drug addict," said her psychologist.

"And all you do is get me addicted to another drug."

"The medication? I doubt it."

"Every human interaction is a burden."

"You can't control another human being."

"Miranda wants Paul to be her father. She craves a father."

"What about you?"

"I don't want to be alone. But not with conditions."

"There are always conditions."

"You make me so mad."

"You pay me for the privilege."

On her way home, she fondled the pack in her purse as though it were a human hand. She cried because she knew she'd always feel vulnerable and there was nothing for it but to feel that way. She stopped at a grocery store and threw her matches and cigarettes into a trashcan.

She called Miranda on her cell phone.

"Throw them out," she told her daughter. "You know where I hide them. All of them."

As she opened the door to the kitchen, Paul was there with his brilliant brown eyes and calm.

They kissed. It was the first time she did not feel the shame of offering to him a mouth filled with ash.

Oblivious, she breathed deeply and gave all her passion to her kisses. She couldn't stop.

REVENGE

Most of the plane's riders wore company overalls, carried their coats, and plugged their ears with bright orange company-issued cylinders of form-fitting sponge. She wore a hooded down coat several sizes too big and fit her small, double-soxed feet into large down-lined boots. Most slept or yakked during the flight, while she gazed at the mountains passing below.

She was met by Joe, who had an edge of shyness one took for granted in a landscape crusted with mostly pristine snow and flat for miles west till one met the mountains or north till one met the ice-floed sea.

Joe carried her bag to the truck still running and plugged into a heater. Protected by a scarf and mittens in addition to the coat and shoes and the long silk underwear she wore under her corduroys, she walked to the dusty truck, barely noticing the sub-zero air. It was a high step up into the springless passenger seat, and a hard slam to the door.

The sun hovered around the horizon for several hours, its light boosted by its reflection off the desolate snow.

When it finally set as they were driving along the carefully designated roads, it was like the end of a long twilight.

They passed by many active rigs, some inactive rigs lying derrick down and ready to be hauled to other locations, and several wells already drilled that were housed in small shacks and whose flow was regulated by a system of valves, meters, and automatic controls. Some of these fed into the Alaska pipeline. Some of these fed into refineries that produced fuel for local trucks and power generators. The North Slope did not have to rely on energy from any other source.

Joe drove her to a brightly lighted building sprawled amid the night.

A silver fox was digging into garbage by the side of a door.

"Shouldn't be there, but some of the guys like to feed them," said Joe. "We're not supposed to make them dependent. Just like the land was still wild with us being here."

It was a huge compound, unlike the small portable living quarters she'd seen near the rigs on the way.

Going into the building, she first noticed him, coming out. Huge, dressed in a white fur coat.

Joe shook his head. "He's been up here since the late sixties. He says the spirit of a bear inhabits his body."

She was silent and stared after the man as he walked by the side of the building and bounded into a truck.

She said good-bye to Joe, registered at the front desk, and got her key. Bathed in heat, she walked the long corridors before reaching her room. It was a mix between a hotel, prison, and college dorm. Two rooms accessed one bathroom. The towels were thin, the beds were thin, the sheets were thin. On the bathroom wall was an ominous contraption she figured you could use to give you an enema.

Her room faced the gym and swimming pool. As she closed the window curtains, she could hear crashing sounds when guys weight-lifting took on too much and had to let go quickly before they buckled.

In her narrow bed she dreamt of the polar bear man walking unabashedly onto the tundra, disturbing the delicate plant life that lay dormant beneath the snow.

He flapped his white fur arms and became the largest, blackest raven, flying—climbing, circling, falling in the frigid air—until a crack of sunlight showed, when he flew into the Earth and disappeared.

In the morning, she found the cafeteria. She thought about the trucks making the long trip up the highway carrying cereal and eggs and coffee and bread—tons of it to make people fat and constipated.

Joe met her at nine. She told him about her dream as he drove her to his ice road.

"Everyone dreams about him once they've seen him," he said.

There was a huge truck spilling water over the road.

She and Joe watched.

"They build up about fifteen inches," he explained. "Fifteen inches of ice between the tundra and the surface."

Then they could trundle a new rig and all the pipe across the frozen marshland without disturbing it.

"It's going to be a good road," he said. "We've been building it for days."

Each layer had to freeze solid before they could pour on the next. And they could only be built in winter.

Not that summer was long. But it was too warm then to make an ice road. In the summer came the little flowers, hordes of black flies, and herds of caribou trekking across the land, avoiding the sinking marshes. Joe's eyes were bright as he described it.

Then it was light all day and people forgot what nighttime was.

Joe lived in Anchorage. In the summer, his wife worked in the garden until three in the morning. He had four children.

"They don't know me." He shook his head.

And he didn't know them. But he knew the silver fox and the ravens that perched miles away in Deadhorse. He was, he believed, their caretaker.

There was a celebration every time he came home.

His oldest boy collected every nation's wildlife stamps. His daughter wanted to be a veterinarian. His wife drew illustrations for children's books about owls or geese or porcupines. Even though most people hunted, Joe and his family did not.

Lately, Joe had stopped eating meat.

He backed his truck and turned around to head for Pumpstation number one. Everyone had to see that, he said.

"You have to have your picture taken in front of it," he said.

So she got to see the lengths of pipe outside the building and the sign under which she stood as Joe snapped her camera at the image of her enveloped in her outsized protection from the cold.

She visited several rigs and spoke with the men about their jobs as directional drillers. She visited a couple of rig floors and even, at one, was photographed with her hands on the controls. Everyone was happy to see her, glad to talk about their work.

One trainee had a black eye and swollen lip. He had gotten into a fight. His one good eye shone as he said he'd seen a silver fox on his way to work. No one had seen a bear that winter, though.

When the sun began to wane, Joe drove her back towards the compound. Dozens of trucks were going in the same direction. Joe was puzzled. He got on his cell phone. After that, he was silent.

"He was found a mile or so from Prudhoe Bay—to the east —in the midst of the tundra," Joe said as they drew up to the compound. "No one would have found him except for three ravens circling above for hours. Someone finally ventured on snowshoes to see what the fuss was about. And there he was, crumpled white in the snow, encircled by blood."

Joe left her to dine alone. All the thickset men and women gathered in the cafeteria and talked quietly. Killed by a bear, perhaps. No one knew for sure.

She was afraid to sleep and dream.

The vision of him, huge and resolute, striding fur-clad across the white-crusted ice: It would never leave her as long as she lived.

INTERVIEW WITH
THE AUTHOR

Q: Is there a story behind the stories? For example, *Revenge* sounds so real, like you're actually there in a human habitat today that's near the Arctic Circle.

A: Yes, I've been to Alaska's North Slope. It was eerie to witness how humans have brought tropical comforts to a frigid environment. But I never know when I start a story where it will lead. I just follow the characters and the situation, getting to know them as my writing reveals them.

Q: Where did the narrator's voice in *Jancy* come from?

A: I really don't know. That story is not based on any memory or event I know of. Although the story of Stanislawow, the Polish town whose Jewish population was decimated during World War II, is, unfortunately, all too real. It's based on a memoir I edited that was printed in installments in a Jewish newspaper.

Q: That's mentioned in *The Arrangement*.

A: Yes. There's a wonderful and excruciating documentary, called *Shoah*, directed by Claude Lanzmann and released in 1985. Lanzmann forces you to hear the voices of perpetrators as well as survivors. These were echoing in my head many years later when I wrote that story.

Q: Is there a particular theme you see reflected in your stories?

A: I'm selecting examples of the various types of short fiction I've written over the years. The theme—if there really needs to be one —is that they're all written by the same person.

Q: You've come to writing fiction relatively late in your life. Why is that?

A: The stories were actually written over a period of decades. I wrote my first short story when I was 13. It was published in my school's yearbook. I've written fiction—including poetry, short stories, and plays—pretty steadily over the years. But I didn't have the luxury of either time or the kind of foolhardy courage I think a writer needs to devote to published writing. I had to work. I was fortunate enough to start my career writing for an industrial newspaper, which led me into a whole world I knew nothing about: machine shops and pipe extrusion and plastics manufacturing. Then I worked at a community hospital, which opened my eyes to the overt and covert racism that had been, was being, and still is being perpetrated in this country.

Q: You're from Canada. How old were you when you came to the US?

A: I was 25. It was a huge wrench to leave my "home and native land." On the surface, Canada and the US appear to be quite alike. But, actually, culturally they're quite different.

Q: How so?

A: Canadians, at least in my experience, react more to subtleties in people's emotional expression than Americans do and therefore, generally, tend to be more low-key, at least in public. I remember when I was growing up, a neighbor's son moved to Buffalo and married an American woman. She was so loud, so unabashedly loud, in public. I cringed. I was embarrassed. Such loudness was, in my experience, something you only expressed in private and only when you were driven to the edge. When my parents got loud, it was terrifying.

Q: How have your industrial writing and journalism informed your fiction?

A: In two primary ways, I think. One is that they forced me to ask open-ended questions, listen intently, take good notes, and respect the limitations of life's Earth-bound reality. The other is that I was invited into work environments few get the chance to witness. And in that sense, I think of myself as having an anthropologist's view of my own society. I've learned it's not enough to have opinions of how you think human society does work or ought to work. You have to delve into our society as it is with the objectivity and rigor of an engineer while retaining the perspective of a humanist.

BOOK CLUB DISCUSSION

General Questions

Which story did you like the most? Why?

Which story did you think was the most original or surprising?

What were some passages that stuck in your mind? Read some out loud.

What do you think you'll remember about this book in the years ahead?

Did you read all the stories at one sitting? Why? Or why not?

Do you think you'll revisit these stories? Why? Or why not?

What Is Art?

How do you think the story answers the question, "What is art?"

Why do you think the painter's work succeeded more than the photographer's?

What questions does this story raise about the nature of human sexuality, gender, and identity?

Friends

How do you think the story is informed by its first paragraph?

Describe the relationship between Judy and Sam. Between Stephen and his mother. Between Stephen and Zach.

Glancing Life

What do you think of this story's writing style? How would you describe it? In what ways does this story differ from the others in this book?

Jancy

What do you think of *Jancy*'s narrator? How would you describe him?

Why do you think the narrator was sometimes glad about what happened to Jancy?

What do you think motivated Brent's hostility toward the narrator?

Slave to Love
Do you think the story's narrator is a "slave to love"?

What do you think is meant by the title?

Behind the Scenes
What do you think the story implies about the nature of acting?

Why do you think the salesclerk violated the store's takeback refund policy?

What do you think the story implies about the nature of sex and love?

The Arrangement
What do you think the title means?

How do you think Simon's decision "ruined" Rebecca's parents?

Smoke and Fire
How does the story's title relate to the main character's struggle?

How does this story help you understand the nature of addiction?

Revenge
What do you think the meaning is of the story's title?

Why do you think the main character is a woman? Try to imagine the main character as a man. How would it impact the story?

ABOUT THE AUTHOR

Robin Beckwith

Born in Canada and living in Texas, Robin is a career published writer. Her background is in the arts. She has acted in more than 20 plays and is a member of Actors' Equity, the actors' union. Her journalistic subjects are wide-ranging, including methane's climate impact, hydraulic fracturing, diving, deep Earth and deep space, the limits of electronics, guar, oil shale, and shale oil. Some of her work can be found listed on ResearchGate. She has also authored book reviews and news stories, as well as worked in communications in the community healthcare, banking, telecommunications, arts, healthcare information systems, oilfield services, and upstream petroleum industries. She earned an Honors BA in English and an MBA, in addition to completing two-thirds of the course requirements for a master's degree in Humanities.

SELECTED WRITINGS OF AN OBSCURE WOMAN

The Obscure Woman presents short stories, poem plays, essays, and poetry, each in a separate volume. At the moment, you have invested in Volume I. Others will be published over the next few years.

Selected Writings Of An Obscure Woman, Volume I: Stories

www.ingramcontent.com/pod-product-compliance
Lightning Source LLC
Chambersburg PA
CBHW032109170626
46808CB00008B/2989

9 781934 005040